Together at the Cabin - With My Best Friend's Father

Together Forever

Alara Knight

Published by Alara Knight, 2024.

This is a work of fiction. Similarities to real people, places, or events are entirely coincidental.

TOGETHER AT THE CABIN - WITH MY BEST FRIEND'S FATHER

First edition. August 23, 2024.

ISBN: 979-8227812773

Written by Alara Knight.

Table of Contents

1 - Emily

I was so looking forward to the weekend with Audrey. She was my BFF from high school, and the only reason I kept coming back to the small town I grew up in on college breaks.

Well, her and her father. But Audrey's father, Michael, was not going to be at their cabin this weekend. It would be just us two girls, sitting in the hot tub, drinking cool wine, and bitching lightheartedly about the problems in our lives.

And I also didn't have to stay at my childhood home and watch my own father slowly drinking himself to death while watching sports on tv 24/7.

My mother died when I was fourteen. A car crash that my father survived. But he had never forgiven himself for her death.

Over the past eight years I had watched him slowly degenerate.

But Audrey's father had kind of taken his place. Giving both of us lifts to and from school and activities, and cooking BBQs at the weekends.

I slowly started spending more and more time in Audrey's house than I had in my own. But I had seen Audrey's father less in the last few years, as both Audrey and myself went off to college. But my thoughts often turned to him. When I would see something stupid or funny, on social media I would share it with him. And he always liked everything that I posted.

But still, I never seemed to outgrow my schoolgirl crush on him. Even now at twenty one, when I was much too old to have a crush on anyone, I still compared every boy I dated to him. Which resulted in not having many second dates.

And no third dates, if you know what I mean.

Not that anything could ever come of my fantasies about Audrey's father. I am sure that he still thinks of both his daughter and me as little girls. So whatever feelings I might have were destined to remain a fantasy.

Not to mention what making a move on her father would do to my relationship with Audrey.

I once again put such thoughts out of my mind as I flick the windscreen wipers to full speed. I am heading up to the cabin in my own car, with Audrey coming along later, and the rain is starting to get very heavy. If it doesn't ease up soon we won't be getting into the outdoor hot tub at the cabin this weekend.

But still, sipping cold wine as we lounge about on the sofas inside the cabin will be nearly as good.

The whole point of the weekend is to just hang out and de-stress. We had both been working hard on our finals. And now that we had both finished our exams we were ready for some relaxation. And what better place than out in the woods with no phone service and no internet to distract us.

"Digital detox" might be all the rage these days. But Audrey's father has been taking us out to his cabin several times a year to "get back to nature" as he calls it, ever since we have known each other. And it's a ritual that we have continued during our college years.

Though these days Michael, Audrey's father, is usually too busy to come with us.

I often wondered what it would be like to "get back to nature" with him.

I sight out loud.

There I go again having all these wild fantasies about my best friend's father.

But, truth be told, my feelings for him is why I have never gotten serious with any of the handful of guys I have dated during my life.

Yes, I was a twenty one year old virgin.

Something I have never revealed even to Audrey. And I could definitely never tell her the reason why.

Once again I push all these thoughts out of my mind and concentrate on driving in the rain. I am using my mother's old car. The one they didn't have the accident in. My father had not replaced his car.

I sigh again thinking about my father. But I have never been able to get him to open up about his feelings. When I come home to check up on him he keeps all the conversations casual and superficial. We never talk about the accident or anything of any importance. Definitely never about our feelings.

I can't help worrying about him. But I have also come to accept that there is not much that I can do to help him either.

Once again I drag myself from my thoughts and back to the present.

I am driving through the small town that is nestled in the valley at the foot of the mountain. It is little more than a main street, still inhabited by mom and pops stores.

I slow down, watching the people scurry back to their cars, huddled against the rain. I even see a couple of the stores closing up early. Looking up at the sky all I can see are angry clouds. I guess not many people are going out shopping in a storm.

As I drive slowly over the bridge at the end of town I look out and see that the river is higher than I can ever remember seeing it before.

The water level is almost up to the level of the roadway in the bridge.

But considering that the rain is so heavy that it is like driving through fog I am not surprised that the river would be so high.

I don't know if it was the wind, or the age of the bridge, but I am sure I feel a few shakes as I drive across.

But soon I am back on solid ground and heading up the single road that runs out of town and up the mountain where the cabin is.

I see a couple of other people on the road. All driving pickup trucks and looking like outdoors people as I catch glimpses of them passing in the rain. They are all heading back down the mountain.

The car skids a little as I take a sharp bend.

I slow down, remembering that the tires are probably nearly as old as the car. I know that my father drives to the store every second day, but that the car is not used for anything else.

I skid again. The rain is so heavy that it is forming a film across the surface of the road.

But I have driven up to the cabin many times. In fifteen minutes I will be safe and dry. And opening the first bottle of wine as I wait for Audrey to join me.

2 - Michael

I give the cabin one last walk through as I prepare to head down the mountain. I definitely don't need to be here while my daughter and her friend, Emily, are hanging out for the weekend.

I glanced out the kitchen window to the hot tub which I've cleaned today. I've put the cover back on because the clouds are rolling in and a light rain had started to fall as I had finished cleaning it. However, now the rain was getting much heavier and I was beginning to doubt if they would get to use the hot tub this weekend.

Thoughts of Emily in a bikini flash across my mind and I briefly fantasize about holding her subtle body in my arms as our bodies intertwine.

Then I chide myself for once again having such inappropriate thoughts about my daughter's best friend. A girl I've known since she was fourteen.

Not that she was fourteen anymore. At twenty one she could give any girl a run for their money. And my thoughts often turned to her. The fact that she shares a constant stream of funny observations, from incorrectly spelled signs to cute puppy pictures on her social media just made her all the more appealing. The combination of a hot body and a sensitive soul is almost irresistible.

But she never mentions any boyfriends. Unlike my daughter's feed, which was full of party photos featuring the steady stream of hot guys my daughter sequentially dates.

All in all, I would much rather Audrey come up to the cabin with Emily than any of those "party people". Not that I can have an opinion on the sex life of my adult daughter. Or her friend, I remind myself as I try to clear thoughts of Emily from my mind.

Let's not follow down that train of thought, I say to myself. Or I will end up sounding like a dirty old man.

Because that is what she must think of me. The father of her best friend. Hardly the object of her romantic interests.

I once again put those thoughts to the back of my mind and head for the front door.

Just as I am opening the door the phone rings.

This far from town there is no phone or internet reception, and I want the girls to be able to call if they need me. So I had a good old fashioned landline put in. Even though the phone company had charged me by the mile for laying the line, it was still cheaper and more reliable than a satellite link.

I also considered it the best of both worlds in terms of connectivity. I am still in contact in the event of an emergency, but there is no distraction from social media or online streaming.

I lift up the receiver.

"Hello," I say, knowing very well that the only person who could be calling was my daughter Audrey.

"Hi, Dad. You're still at the cabin," she says.

"Don't worry I'm just on my way down," I reply

"Oh, I didn't mean it like that," Audrey says. "You're more than welcome to stay for the weekend." I can hear the smile in her voice.

"I'd just be in the way," I reply. "But why are you calling?"

"I was just wondering if Emily was there yet," Audrey says. "She said she was going to head up today."

"No, there's no sign of her yet." I find myself looking out the window to check if a car is pulling up.

"Oh, it was just that I was texting her, and she's not replying," Audrey says.

"Well, you know you lose signal as soon as you round the mountain," I say. "That still leaves another hour of driving to get up here."

"Oh, that's probably it," she says.

"Do you want me to leave a message?" I ask.

"No. It's nothing that won't wait until I see her tomorrow," Audrey replies.

"Ok," I say.

"See you later," Audrey replies and hangs up.

I put the phone down.

Before I go I decide to switch on all the exterior lights to welcome Emily. Dusk has already fallen and the sky is full of darkening clouds. She will need the lights just to find her way inside. Especially if this rain gets any heavier.

Satisfied that all is well I lock the door and slip the key under the mat.

Not the most secure place to put it. But if anyone did stumble across a cabin this isolated they would be more likely to be in need of shelter and rescue than be trying to burgle the property.

I climb into my truck and head down the narrow track to the main access road.

3 - Emily

The car skidded again.

I grip the wheel and fight to keep the car on the road. Slowing down yet again as I manage to avoid going into the ditch.

The rain pelted down onto the car and my windscreen wipers are going on full speed trying to keep my windshield clear.

In the headlights, the dirt road looks like a river of mud as the rain pours down onto it and the tires of my mother's old Honda keep losing their grip.

Once again thoughts of the crash that had taken my mother's life come unbidden to my mind. Not that there were any similarities with tonight.

Back then a drunk driver had sped through a red light and hit my parents' car. It was all over before anyone knew it was happening. My mother was killed instantly. And despite there being nothing he could have done, I don't think my father has ever forgiven himself for surviving when my mother died.

But tonight, despite my father looking after the car all these years, I am not sure the old bird is up to the task of fighting the storm. I don't want to get stranded by the side of the road in this weather, that's for sure.

But I'm not sure how far I have come. Would it be quicker to turn around and head back down to town? Or am I closer to the cabin?

Also, Audrey is coming up in her own car and I am not sure if she has already left home. I wouldn't want to leave her all alone for the weekend. Not when I have all the bottles of wine in a box on my back seat.

Yet another bend looms out of the darkness ahead.

I swear, in the sunshine, this is the most pleasant of drives. Especially in Audrey's convertible, with the top down and the wind in our hair, and the sunshine sparkling through the trees.

But tonight I feel like I'm trapped in some kind of horror movie.

I'm even driving to a cabin in the woods!

I smile to myself as I think about this. This cabin was like a second home to me and Audrey all through our high school years. Her father would drive us up most weekends during the summer, and even in the winter.

I used to feel so high up riding in the cabin of his big pickup truck.

He was always in control of these narrow roads, with a sure hand on the wheel as he drove effortlessly along the twisty mountain roads. I used to feel so safe with him behind the wheel.

But tonight I sigh as I struggle to keep my car from skidding.

It's summertime, so at least the rain isn't icy cold, I think to myself.

My phone pings three times in quick succession, startling me as I wasn't expecting to have any coverage up here.

On the road ahead I see a safe place to pull in. I keep my lights on and the engine running as I put on the parking brake. While the road is straight for about one hundred yards here, it is still on a steep incline.

I have two texts saying I have voicemail, and a third from Audrey.

I swipe it open and see that she is asking if I have left for the cabin yet.

I text back that I am almost at the cabin and will soon be safe and dry.

When I hit send the refresh circle spins, and spins, for the longest time before it stops. I can only assume that the message has been sent.

I put the car back into drive and pull out slowly. I'm not expecting any cars to come racing up the road behind me, but the road surface is slick with the rain and I don't want to skid into a tree.

The rain is still getting heavier and I wonder again if it would be safer to turn back. There are no longer any other cars on the road.

There had been quite a few at first, mostly trucks and all heading down the mountain. But as I climbed higher the other traffic had disappeared.

"Maybe they know something I don't," I whisper to myself as I gingerly guide my car around another bend. "Perhaps I should turn back."

But just then another car comes down the road towards me. Its headlights illuminate the sheets of rain that blow between us as we pass by each other. It too is driving slowly in the rain. But at least that driver is in a big, four wheel drive pickup.

"Well, if there are other people up here I guess it can't be as bad as all that," I reassure myself as I decide to press on, carefully taking the next bend.

Then in my headlights I see an old oak tree that I recognize. And I smile to myself. The cabin is only five minutes away. I relax a little.

But the back of the car swings out and I am suddenly moving sideways.

I turn the wheel, steering into the skid to regain control as the car floats sideways across the road.

I hope there isn't another car about to come around the bend, as I am now on the wrong side of the road.

My tires find some grip and I manage to straighten the car.

But it is too late.

The last thing I see is that old oak tree rushing towards me.

And then with an almighty crashing sound everything goes black.

4 - Michael

The cabin is fully stocked for the weekend, I think to myself as I slow down to take a steep bend. But as I look out at torrential rain I doubt that either of the girls will want to come up to the cabin for the weekend.

This storm came out of nowhere. All that had been forecast was "heavy rain", but the phrase "heavy rain" did not do this deluge any justice. Even in my 4-wheel drive truck I am having trouble keeping straight on the slick roads tonight. I worry about either of the girls driving their little, city hatchbacks on these steep, unpaved roads.

A storm warning had come over the radio as I left the cabin, so it was going to be a wet and windy weekend, and I was glad I was heading back down the mountain.

And I am not the only one heading for cover. By now, I am the only one left on this narrow mountain road. The only other car I meet on my way down the Mountain is an old Honda. I hope they are not going very far because the roads have become treacherous in the rain. There must be at least an inch of water flowing across the packed dirt. Turning the surface more into a muddy stream than a road with a driveable surface.

Back down in the valley the roads are better surfaced, but the rain is still making them slippery.

I pull out of the side road and onto the main road into Smithfield, the nearest town to my cabin, nestled beside a river on the floor of the valley.

On the approach to the town the road runs parallel to the river. Normally the water is quiet and meandering. But today it is a raging torrent that threatens to overflow its banks and flood the road.

Down here I can at least get a signal, on my phone.

I phone my daughter to tell her not to bother coming up to the cabin.

"Hi, dad." My daughter answers her phone.

"Hi, Audrey," I reply. "I'm on my way down from the cabin."

"Everything is all set for our weekend I hope," she says.

"Listen, sweetly," I say. "I don't think you'll be getting up to the cabin tomorrow. Or even the next few days. A storm has come in and the roads are treacherous."

"Oh, that's too bad." I can hear the disappointment in her voice. "We were looking forward to hanging out for the weekend."

"Well, you can still hang at home," I say.

"Yeah," Audrey replies.

"I know it's not the same," I say. "But I promise to stay out of your way."

"Oh, don't be silly, dad," Audrey says. "You're never in the way."

I laugh in response.

"Anyway, I still haven't been able to reach Emily," Audrey says. "She had set off a couple of hours again, planning on spending tonight alone, before I go up tomorrow."

"A couple of hours ago?" I ask, concerned. The thought of Emily on the mountain in this weather alarms me.

"What car was she driving?" I ask.

"She usually takes her mother's old Honda," Audrey replied.

I remember the Honda I saw on my way down. A knot of fear forms in the pit of my stomach.

"She should be on her way up now," Audrey says. "I had texted her a few minutes ago, but I assumed she didn't reply because she is driving."

I really want to turn back and check if Emily is safe.

But then I don't know for sure that it was Emily in that car.

"Yeah, sure," I reply. "I'll see you when I get home."

"Yeah. See you, dad." And she hangs up.

I turn a corner and see that the river has in fact overflowed its banks and is spilling out across the road. I slow down, but my truck can easily handle the six inches of water.

Well, it's six inches at the moment, but it looks as if the river is continuing to swell.

I assume that if Emily had seen this flooding that she would have had the sense to turn back.

"At least I hope she would have the sense to turn back," I say to myself.

I didn't like the idea of Emily being alone at the cabin for the weekend.

then the thought of being trapped alone with her at the cabin flashed across my mind. It was on the one hand an appealing prospect. But on the other hand, I didn't think I could control myself being in such close quarters with her for the whole weekend. Alone.

It is not that I wouldn't be able to control myself physically. The fear I have is that I would reveal my feelings and make a fool of myself.

Not only make a fool of myself, but also ruin my relationship with Emily. And Emily's relationship with my daughter.

Around the next bend I come to the bridge that crosses the river. It is the only way in and out of town if you want to head up the mountain.

But I pull to a stop before driving onto it.

The river is higher than I have ever seen. The water is not just surging around the pylons, but also splashing up onto the deck of the bridge.

The bridge itself is twisted. The two supports in the middle are no longer vertical. And the structure is making a low wailing sound.

It does not look as if the bridge is going to be able to resist the raging waters for very long.

I sit there for a few minutes and watch as the bridge slowly tilts over, the metal and wood bending and twisting under the strength of the water.

Then with one ear splitting screech the bridge collapses into the water and most of it is washed away within seconds.

And I am left staring at the washed out remains of the bridge.

I hit redial on my phone and a moment later Audrey answers.

"Hi, Sweety," I say. "I have some bad news. The bridge out of Smithfield has been washed away."

"Washed away!" Audrey asks. "But what about Emily?"

"Don't worry, Audrey," I say. "There was no one on the bridge when it collapsed."

"But she's out of coverage. That must mean that she is on the mountain," Audrey says.

"Yes," I reply, there was no doubt that it was her car that I passed.

"I hope she's going to be alright all alone at the cabin," Audrey says.

The thought of Emily being alone in this storm made my stomach clench in fear. "I am going to go back up and check in on her." I sit and watch as the last piling gives way and the remains of the bridge are lost to the flooding water.

"That would be good," my daughter replies. "You will take care of her, won't you?"

I banish the ways I want to take care of Emily from my mind as I look up the valley at the town. The lights flicker once and then go dead as the power goes out.

Now the only light is from my headlights.

"Of course I'll look after her," I say.

But there is no response.

"Hello," I say into my phone. "Audrey, Audrey are you there?"

But the connection is dead

"Fuck!" I say, as I slam my truck into reverse and turn to head back to the cabin. Fear and worry clawing at my gut as I drive into the dark and stormy night.

5 - Emily

I wake up with a sore head. And the taste of blood in my mouth.

I am lying awkwardly against something hard. And my whole body aches.

The white noise of heavy rain hitting a tin roof surrounds me. And I realize that I am still in the car.

I push myself up and find that I had been lying against the steering wheel of the car.

I try to sit back against the car seat, but find that the car is at a sharp angle facing down.

I remember the car going into a skid and realize that I have ended up in a ditch.

Outside both side windows is pitch blackness, with the lights from my dashboard reflecting in the glass and illuminating the rain as it cascades down my windows.

The only light is ahead of me, where the one remaining headlight shows a thick tangle of undergrowth pressed tight up against the front of my car.

My shoulder is sore from where the seat belt stopped me from flying through the windscreen. I switch on the cabin light and look at myself in the mirror. I have a big bruise above my eye, but there is no blood anywhere to be seen.

I pat myself down and move my legs and feet and find that nothing is broken.

I breathe a big sigh of relief. It could have been much worse.

But what shall I do now?

I don't think waiting for rescue is a good choice. I look up and down the road, out the side windows. But there is nothing to be seen but darkness in every direction.

The engine is still running. So moving the car seems the best option.

I slip the car into reverse and give it some gas. I can hear the engine revving and the tires turning, but while the car shakes a bit it doesn't move even an inch.

I try again, pumping the gas pedal, and even rocking back and forth in my seat. But I quickly stop when I hear a loud squeal and the front of the car drops down another few inches.

I put the car into park and take a deep breath. I am obviously stuck and the car is going nowhere.

Considering how remote I am, and with the storm blowing outside, I am not hopeful that anyone is going to come along and find me any time soon.

I suppose I should just wait in the car. But I can't help but think that maybe the car will explode.

I laugh, but I kill the engine, just in case. Then I carefully sniff the air. Luckily I can't smell any gas or burning plastic. But still, I am not comfortable staying in a crashed car.

I am dressed in a t-shirt and leggings but I have a heavy coat with my bag in the trunk.

Looking at the rain running in thick waves down the windows I know I am going to get soaked as soon as I get out of the car.

The car is a hatchback, so I suppose I could climb over the front seats, and pull the back seats down to get at the stuff in the trunk. But that seems like a bit of an extreme move.

Instead, I flip on the flashlight on my phone and open the car door.

It is only as I am opening the door that I wonder if it might be jammed from the crash. But it swings open. A bit too quickly as a gust of wind catches it, and with the aid of gravity I am almost flung out of the car and into the ditch.

But I catch myself as the door opens fully, and the car shakes and slips even deeper into the ditch.

I jump out of my seat, fearing that the car is about to slip further down the mountain. And I am immediately ankle deep in ice cold water.

Clambering through the interior of the car doesn't seem like such a silly idea now.

I climb out of the ditch, soaking my hands and knees in ice cold mud as I do so, and finally gain some solid footing as I make it onto the road.

My phone shows that the rear wheels are several inches off the ground. And even as I stand there beside it the car shakes and sinks even further into the ditch.

Quickly I move around to the back of the car and pop the hatchback.

Already I am soaked to the skin with ice cold water. The kind of rain that sucks the heat right out of your body.

Inside the trunk everything has been thrown about. But the light from my phone shows me the coat and I quickly grab it and put it on.

I feel some heat now, even if my clothes underneath are still soaking wet.

It is a heavy coat, with a big hood on it. So at least I won't die of hypothermia now.

But the next question is where should I go?

I've already decided that I cannot stay in the car. Standing around in the rain is just going to get me wet. Which scares me more than sitting inside the car sheltering from the rain. So that leaves me with a choice of walking somewhere.

I look up and down the road. But there is nothing but blackness and rain in every direction.

I lean forward into the car to shelter my phone from the rain and tap on the map icon.

Luckily I have dropped a pin at the cabin and my phone still has GPS even if I don't have cell service.

The pin looks to be very close by. I'll turn around, trying to orientate myself in the correct direction. The straight path to the pin leads across the road and up into a tangle of undergrowth and trees. I would rather walk along the road, just to be clear of obstructions. But I know that the road takes a long, and winding, route around the mountain and will be much longer than walking directly uphill.

That way I can get out of these wet clothes and into a hot shower sooner, I reason with myself.

While I'm heading for an isolated cabin in the wilderness, Michael has no problem with all of the modern conveniences. The cabin is connected to the electricity grid, and he also has a battery backup and solar panels on the roof. So that they can live off grid in, as he says, "The event of any emergencies."

So I know they'll be hot water for a hot shower and also plenty of food at the cabin. My stomach starts to rumble.

I look at the map on my phone once again. And hope that my phone is "water resistant" because even leaning forward into the hatchback of the car for shelter my phone is already splashed with raindrops.

I set off uphill, mustering as much positivity as I can.

But it is not long before. I start to regret my decision. Every step seems to push me ankle deep into ice cold mud. The branches claw at my legs and my arms and even at my face, I keep my head down and pull my head as far forward as I can. But my hands are getting frozen, and I am afraid that I might let my phone slip out of my grip.

But I feel it is too late to turn back now. While I have a pin to show me where the cabin is, I doubt there is any way I can make it through the dark forest back to the car. I'll look around in every direction, but there's nothing else but the dark and wet night around me.

So I brace myself as best I can and push forward into the tangle of wet branches and leaves.

Suddenly I feel a sharp twist of pain. And my right ankle gives way, throwing me face first into a tangle of undergrowth.

6 - Michael

I am over three quarters of the way back to the cabin when I find Emily's car.

It is crunched into an old oak tree that had been hit by lightning many years ago.

My heart skips a beat as I skid to a stop and jump out of my truck, terrified of what I might find inside as I dash through the rain to the car.

One of the headlights is on, but the engine is not running. The driver's door is open and there is no sign of Emily anywhere.

I breathe a sigh of relief at not finding her injured, or worse.

But then I feel the panic rising again. Where is she?

"Emily!" I call out. "Emily! Where are you!"

I look around.

But there is nothing to see outside the pools of light from the two sets of headlights.

"Emily!" I call again as I fish my phone out of my pocket.

But there is no signal up here.

"Emily!" I call again, looking up and down the mountain, trying to figure which way she would have gone.

"Up to the cabin! Of course," I say. That makes the most sense.

I grab a heavy duty flashlight from my truck. And also slip a smaller one into my pocket, just in case.

Turning back to the forest I switch the flashlight to a wide beam and jump over the ditch that Emily's car is in.

I duck inside to check that the car is empty. But there is no one inside. I leave the headlights on. A flat battery in the morning was a small price to pay for leaving the lights on in case someone else did come along this mountain road in the dead of night.

I close the car door and jump back onto the road, looking around once again for any sign of Emily. But between the rain and the undergrowth the beam from my flashlight did not reach very far.

"Emily!" I call out once more. "Emily!"

My heart is beating in my chest. The thought of her being out in this torrential downpour was tearing me apart. Especially as I just knew she wouldn't be dressed for the weather.

I close the hatchback of her car and turn to face uphill.

Once again I call out. But once again there is no answer.

So I once again jump over the ditch by the side of the road and push my way into the dense undergrowth.

I call out as I go, trying to keep a straight line from the road. The cabin should be more or less directly uphill from the crash site. And once you got close the lights I'd left on should be visible, even through the thick growth of vegetation.

She had almost made it all the way up to the cabin before her car hit the tree. Which was good going considering the old set of summer tires that I noticed on her car.

But walking along the road would have been a better choice than trying to make her way through this tangle of wild undergrowth in the pitch dark and the pouring rain.

Though I don't suppose that she knew how close she had gotten to the cabin.

I duck under a thick branch and as I straighten up I call out her name once again.

"Emily!" My voice doesn't seem to carry very far with the noise of the rain in the dense forest.

But I call out again, "Emily!"

I am starting to get very wet. Even my heavy duty boots are starting to let the rain in.

I hadn't thought that she would have gotten this far and now I was beginning to worry once again.

"Emily!" I call out again, as loudly as I can.

"Over here." I hear a faint voice over the sound of the wind and the rain.

"Emily!" I call, trying to find the source of the voice.

"Over here," she calls again. And I see a light flashing through the trees.

"Emily." I head straight towards her. Crashing through the undergrowth and crunching fallen branches under my boots.

"Michael," she replies, sounding confused.

"Emily," I reply, as I push through one final tangle of branches.

She is sitting on the ground. Soaked to the skin. The flashlight from her phone illuminating her right leg which is stretched out in front of her.

"Are you alright?" I ask. Seeing her sprawled on the cold, wet ground seemed to twitch my heart in my chest. "What happened?" I kneel beside her, automatically putting my arm on her shoulder.

"I kind of hurt my ankle," she says.

"Emily." My heart melts as I kneel beside her. "Your ankle?" I reach down but stop just short of touching her.

Her foot is aligned with her leg and there are no obvious signs of a break.

And, thankfully, no blood.

I give her a quick look over, just to make sure.

But apart from some scratches on her hands there are no signs of injuries.

"Are you ok?" I repeat, as I finally look at her face.

"Yes," she smiles. "Now that you're here."

I don't catch her meaning as I am still concerned, hypothermia could still set in. And her ankle.

"Where does it hurt?" I ask.

"It's just my ankle," she replies. "And my pride."

I gently touch her ankle and relax a little when I find no broken bones.

"What did you think you were doing?" I ask.

"My car went off the road," she replies. "And I thought the cabin was just up the hill a little."

I looked at her face and she continued sheepishly, "And I thought I could walk it."

"Walk it? In this weather?" I ask.

"Well, I..."

"It's ok," I say. "I'm here now."

"Yes," she smiles again.

"Let's get you up and back to my truck," I say, as I wrap one arm around her.

"Here, hold this." I give her my flashlight and then hook my other arm under her legs and lift her up.

I look around a moment to get my bearings, then head off to the left where I see a break in the trees.

As I had hoped, the road was only about six feet away and the undergrowth was not too thick.

"Oh, I didn't get very far," Emily says, as we step out onto the road.

"The road curves back around," I explain.

"Maybe I should have stuck to the road," she says.

"Yes," I reply. "That would have been the sensible choice." I am both annoyed that she thought crashing about in the forest in the middle of a storm was a good idea. And relieved that I found her safe and relatively sound.

7 - Emily

I feel so foolish when he easily picks me up and turns to carry me back to his truck.

But then I start to feel something else as he holds me close. There is a certain safety and comfort to being carried through the dark and rainy night by such a strong man. I feel like a little girl in his arms. And my thoughts start to stray. I start to feel a little bit flushed even under my soaking wet clothes.

But then I return to feeling foolish again, when about thirty seconds after he picks me up Michael carries me out of the trees and back onto the road. Where, directly in front of us, is my crashed car and his big truck, not twenty feet from where I had fallen with my twisted ankle.

So much for showing off how much of an outdoorswoman I am, I think to myself as he opens the passenger door and slides me onto the seat.

He quickly checks that I am sitting comfortably, and even fastens the seat belt around me, before he closes the door. I just sit there as he comes around to the driver's side, not knowing how I should feel.

On the one hand, as soon as the door is closed I breathe a big sigh of relief at being out of the rain. It is hard to imagine just how heavy the rain is until I was safely out of it.

But on the other hand, I am anxious, maybe scared, definitely excited at the idea of finally being alone with Michael. Not that anything is going to happen, for I am quite sure that I am much too young for him. What forty four year old man would be interested in a twenty two year old girl? He is literally twice my age.

But, then again, I can't remember the last time I was alone with Michael.

In fact, I might never have been alone with Michael. Every time I was at his house I was visiting with Audrey. It's not like we've ever dated. So I don't think we have ever been alone together in my entire life.

And now he is walking around to the driver's seat and we are definitely going to be alone together. Alone together halfway up a mountain in the pitch dark and the pouring rain, with not another live soul around for miles.

I try to banish these foolish thoughts from my mind. I mean, I think I've been foolish enough for one day.

Michael climbs into the driver's seat and before he even closes his door he is turning the heat up to full blast.

I hadn't realized just how cold I was until the hot air hit my wet skin.

"Oh, thank you, Michael," I sigh, luxuriating in the heat.

"No problem," he replies. "But the bridge to Smithfield is out."

"Out?" I ask.

"Washed away by the storm waters." He turns to look at me.

"But what about Audrey?" I ask. I look out the window. But all I can see is rain. "Is she already at the cabin?"

"Audrey is not going to be making it up to the cabin any time soon," he replies as he puts the truck into gear.

"Oh, I reply. I had been excited, or scared, or whatever about being alone with Michael while we drove to the cabin. And maybe even alone for an hour or two more while we waited for Audrey to join us. But now it is going to be just the two of us alone for the entire night. Maybe just the two of us alone for the entire weekend. Now my excitement, and my foolish fantasies, were causing feelings of anxiety.

Not that I had any fear of Michael. Despite his rugged good looks I knew he was a perfect gentleman. I couldn't imagine him hurting a fly. And while he had a cabin in the woods he didn't even fish, never mind hunt. So I had no fear of this gentle giant.

No, what I was most afraid of was revealing my foolish fantasies to him. How would he react if he knew how I felt about him.

I had always told myself, once I realized that I had these feelings for him, that I would grow out of it. That it was just a phase. A puppy love crush on my best friend's father. But even though I dated casually during high school, and college, one of the reasons I never went on more than one or two dates with any boy was because I really wanted to be dating Michael.

My feelings for him colored every aspect of my life.

Not that Audrey and I wouldn't have been the best of friends if I didn't like her father. She was the sister that I never had. In fact her and Michael were the only stable family I have known in years.

But, as I said, it was always her and Michael.

She was always there to act as a buffer between us.

And I can't imagine that Michael would see me as anything other than a little girl.

But without Audrey to dominate the conversation, what was I going to talk to Michael about? I faced a whole weekend of small talk, when all I really wanted to say to him was how I felt about him.

It was bound to slip out some time, somehow. I wouldn't be able to keep my feelings in check with nothing else between us while we are basically trapped together in a cabin in the woods.

All these thoughts collided around in my head during the drive up to the cabin.

Michael drove slowly, keeping his eyes on the road and his thoughts to himself.

I just sat and stewed in my own thoughts.

This was going to be a disaster.

Once he knew how I felt about him he would never want to be near me again.

There would be no more "sleepovers" with Audrey. No more summer BBQs. No more weekends at the cabin.

His cabin.

Where he was taking me now. And which I would never see again once I came down from the mountain.

And I would never see Michael again either.

8 - Michael

And so, the one thing that I definitely didn't want to happen is going to happen.

Emily and I are going to be spending at least one night, if not several nights, alone at the cabin, together.

I think about the logging trail that runs down the other side of the mountain. In good weather I could definitely make it with my truck. But after a downpour like the one we're having at the moment, I'm not sure even the logging company would send men up the mountain until the mudslides dry out.

No, I sigh to myself, we are going to be spending some time together.

I glance across at Emily. She is looking out the window

I'll just have to man up and control myself, I say to myself, as I turn my eyes back to the road. The last thing I want is to hurt this precious little girl.

I glance across again and catch her eye reflected in the window.

Was she looking at me?

The truck skids as we take a bend and I fight the wheel as the truck threatens to lose its grip on the road.

Emily gasps.

"It's OK," I reassure her, as I get the truck under control once again. "This truck can handle much worse than this storm."

"That's good to know," Emily smiles. "One crash a night is more than enough."

I smile back and from then on I try to concentrate on not getting us both killed before we get to the cabin. But her presence in my truck is not something that I can ignore.

Like a moth to a candle, my thoughts keep coming to her. And to the fantasies that I have of making her mine and protecting her for the rest of her life.

Luckily the cabin is not that far and soon we are driving up the last stretch of road. Though the road is more a track at this point. And the truck bounces from side to side as the wheels churn through the mud and roll over rocks in the last few hundred yards.

But I can see the bright lights of the cabin shining out of the gloom ahead of us and I know that soon we will be safe and dry.

"Wow," Emily says. "That's a sight for sore eyes." She smiles across at me

"It certainly is," I smile back.

Our gaze lingers for a moment.

Until the truck hits a pothole and I return my concentration to getting up the last one hundred yards in one piece.

I pull to a stop with the passenger door as close to the cabin as I can.

"You wait here while I unlock the cabin," I say, as I kill the engine.

"OK," she says.

I jump out of the truck and dash across to the cabin, quickly retrieving the key from under the doormat and unlocking the front door.

When I had locked the cabin earlier that night I had thought that the only people needing to use the cabin would be those in need of rescue. I had never thought that it would be me that was going to be rescuing Emily.

But we were not quite there yet.

I turned and dashed back out into the downpour.

By the time I take the few steps back to the truck I can already feel a new stream of ice cold water soaking into my shirt.

I open the passenger door and reach in, popping her seatbelt before lifting her up in my arms once again.

"We'll have to make a quick dash for it," I say as I swing around and kick the door closed.

Four quick steps and we are finally out of the storm and into the cabin.

As I carry her inside, I can't help but think that I am carrying her over the threshold, like a newlywed in an old movie. And once again I tell myself to control my fantasies before I ruin our friendship.

As gently as I can I place her on the couch in front of the fire. Then I quickly close and lock the cabin door, shutting the storm outside.

It is only as I am locking the door that I realize that I did not take Emily's luggage from her car.

I don't have any luggage. I hadn't been planning on staying. I have a bunch of clothes that I leave up here in the cabin. So I will be alright.

But now I wonder what Emily will wear. The clothes she has on her are soaked. She will have to change.

When I turn back to her I can see that she is shivering with cold.

"Let me get this fire going," I say, as I rush across to the fireplace.

Luckily I have already set the fire and it only takes a moment for the kindling to catch and the fire to take hold.

Within moments heat is flooding the cabin.

"Blankets," I say as I turn back to Emily. "And towels."

As I rush out to get the aforementioned items I can feel Emily smiling at my sudden awkwardness.

9 - Emily

Michael comes back with an enormous bundle of blankets and towels. They make quite a thud as he drops them on the floor beside me. Before I can even draw a breath he has pulled out a big fluffy towel and is wrapping it around my shoulders rubbing at my soaked hair.

"Okay, okay," I say with a smile. "Can I at least get my coat and shoes off first? "

"Em, yes. Of course," he replies, taking half a step backwards.

He hovers over me as I pull my coat off.

I hand it to him and he pulls a dining chair around and hangs the coat on the back of it facing the fire, to dry.

"Luckily I don't have boots on," I say as I pull my sneakers off. I feel a twinge of pain as I pull the right sneaker off.

"If you had proper hiking boots on you might not have twisted your ankle in the first place," Michael says.

"Well, I was planning on driving, not walking," I reply.

"Yes, of course. Sorry," he replies, kneeling down to look at my ankle.

He is so gentle as he pulls the dripping wet sock from my foot and carefully presses his fingers into my skin, examining my ankle.

"Definitely nothing broken," he says. "But it will be tender for a few days."

"I don't think I'll be walking anywhere far for the next day or two," I smile, as I nod towards the rain pelting against the windows.

"Um, no. I guess not," Michael glances at the windows, but had a more serious look on his face. "Let's get you a bandage for your ankle."

"I don't think it's that bad," I say, wiggling my toes. "It's more my pride than my ankle that's been hurt."

"Oh, don't be silly," he replies. "Anyone can have an accident." He smiles at me, and adds, "or two."

I smile back as I say, "Thanks."

"But seriously, let me at least get you some painkillers." He stands and heads out to the kitchen. "And maybe an ice pack," he calls over his shoulder.

"Maybe not an ice pack," I call back, still shivering with the cold.

I hear him laugh as he opens a cupboard in the kitchen.

In moments he is back with a glass of soda and a couple of painkillers.

"Thanks," I say, as I take them from his hands, and swallow the tablets with a big gulp of soda.

He once again hovers over me, watching as I take the tablets. It is at once endearing and frustrating. Endearing, because he obviously cares for me. But also frustrating as I want him to do much more than hover. Ever so much more.

"How do you feel?" he asks.

"Much better now that I'm out of the storm," I say. "But I do need to get out of these wet clothes."

As I speak I am acutely aware that we are alone in the cabin and I am talking about getting naked.

"Your clothes," he says. "I didn't even think to grab your stuff from the car."

"Oh," I say.

"Maybe I should go back." He looks towards the door.

"No!" I say. It is an instinctive exclamation.

He looks at me.

"I mean," I say. "I don't want to be left alone in the cabin. And there's no need to go out in the storm for a few changes of clothes." I didn't mention the bottles of wine I had packed for Audrey and myself to enjoy.

"No, I guess not," he says. "But still..."

"I'm sure Audrey must have some spare clothes in her room," I say. I go to stand, but wince at the pain from my ankle.

Michael steps forward, arms outstretched to catch me.

But I am sitting down again before he reaches me.

"Maybe I shouldn't walk," I say.

"No," he agrees.

"Would you go and look for me?" I ask.

"Em," he looks towards the door into Audrey's bedroom. "Are you sure?"

"Yes," I reply. "Go check."

"OK," he says.

"I'll wrap myself in blankets while I wait," I say.

"Ok," he repeats, and walks into Audrey's bedroom.

At first it was a little awkward to start to undress in the living room when Michael could return at any moment. But I hear him bandaging about in Audrey's bedroom and I know that I have a few minutes before he'll return.

But I am soaked to the skin. Every item of my clothing is soaked.

I was planning on leaving my underwear on, but there was no way that I can when everything is so wet.

I reach into the big pile that must consist of every towel in the cabin and pull out a big bath towel. Which I drape over my shoulders as I shrug off my T-shirt and bra, both soaked.

Next, I wrap another towel around my body and, being careful not to put any weight on my twisted ankle, I scooch up and pull down my leggings and panties, slipping another towel under me as I sit back down.

I am just tucking a big bath towel around myself when Michael comes back.

"Oh, sorry," he says, as he pauses in the doorway.

"It ok," I reply, as I clamp my elbows to my sides to stop the towel from slipping.

"Em, the cupboards were bare." He holds up a skimpy bathrobe and some cropped t-shirts.

"Oh," I say, thinking I might be spending the weekend wrapped in towels.

"The only other things I found were swimwear," he says. "I'm not sure if you want those."

I smile. "No," I say. "I don't think I need to hang out in one of Audrey's bikinis."

He smiles. But I swear he blushes too.

"No, of course," he says.

He drops the items from Audrey's room onto the couch and walks into the other bedroom.

Presumably his bedroom.

He leaves the door open and I hear him moving about, but cannot see what he is doing. Until moments later he returns with a handful of plaid shirts and a couple of tracksuit bottoms.

"These are definitely going to be too big for you," he says. "But they'll be a lot better than towels."

I look down at the shirts, his shirts, and then smile up at him.

"They will do just fine," I say.

"Good," he smiles back.

I feel weird sitting on the couch wrapped in half a dozen big bath towels.

And once again Michael is hovering.

Then I realize that he is still soaking wet.

"You're still soaking wet," I say. "Go shower and change before you catch pneumonia."

"Um, yes," he replies. "I guess I'd better."

He heads back into his bedroom.

And as I pick up one of his plaid shirts, a naughty smile spreads across my face.

10 - Michael

I cannot get the image of Emily sitting on the couch wrapped in wet towels out of my mind. I close the door to my bedroom, but that doesn't seem like a big enough barrier to control my deepest impulses. I want to rip the flimsy towels from her soft skin and hold her tight to me as I warm her with my body heat.

I quickly stripped off my own wet clothes. And find myself standing naked staring at the door with my hard cock squeezed tightly in my hand. I hand squeezing my erect cock so hard that it almost hurts. My fingers are wrapped around the shaft so tight that I am on a hair trigger, about to come at any moment.

I take a couple of deep, deep breaths and try to calm myself. Finally I manage to tear myself away and go into the master ensuite, smashing at the shower controls to make the water start flowing.

I stand there in the cold water waiting for it to warm up but I can still not clear my head.

The girl that I want, the only girl I've wanted for such a long time, is sitting practically naked not 10 feet from where I am. And there is nothing that I can do about it.

I want to how and for striation and scream into the wind that I can hear nothing around the cabin outside the cabin.

I take some more deep breaths and try to calm myself, as I let the hot water cascade over cold skin. Soothing away some of the tension that I feel.

I concentrate on the sensations of the water flowing over my head and down my body. My hands are pressed hard against the wall. I do not trust myself to move them.

I do not want to jack off to my memories of Emily. As I have often done in the past.

Maybe, way too often.

More often than I would ever admit to it, at any rate.

But not when she was mere feet away from me. that would be just too much to bear.

But still, I cannot forget that her delicious body is sitting outside my bedroom door, practically served to me on a plate, and I fight to control myself.

There is no way I could ever betray my friendship with her. There is no way I can ever expose my true feelings to her. For her to reject me will be more than I could bear.

So instead I shall just man up and learn to control myself.

There is nothing else that I can do.

But then the hum of the extractor fan cuts off. And the cascade of water comes to a stop. I open my eyes and realize that I am in pitch darkness.

The storm must have cut the power supply.

A surge of panic runs through my body. Emily is alone in the dark.

I turn and fumble for a moment with the shower door. Then I'm feeling for the towel rail in the dark. I grab a towel and head out into my bedroom.

There is a window in my bedroom giving me faint light that allows me to orientate myself towards the door. But I still manage to smash my shin against the bed as I walk across the room. I curse under my breath, hopping for a moment in pain, before returning to my mission.

I pull open my bedroom door and rush outside.

"It's okay Emily. It's just a power going off," I say, before coming to a dead stop as I see Emily calmly sitting on the sofa, brightly illuminated by the light of the roaring fire that I had lit for her.

The image takes my breath away and I stand still, dumbfounded.

She is the most beautiful and serene sight that I have ever seen.

Feelings that I have been trying to repress, not just for this evening, but for as long as I can remember, come rushing through my whole body.

I feel my flesh tremble with desire. And I am frozen in front of her, unable to do or say a single thing.

But the one thing that I do realize is that my raging erection has returned.

And Emily is staring directly at it.

A moment later I snap to my senses and try to pull the towel around my waist.

But in my haste, and the darkness, I had grabbed a hand towel and not a bath towel. So there was not much towel to wrap around myself.

I see a smile curling at the corners of her luscious lips.

A smile, and something else in her eyes as she openly regards me.

Then she does something I would never have expected she'd do in a million years.

11 - Emily

I have just finished artfully arranging one of his big plaid shirts around myself. It really is big enough on me to be a dress. Of course I was naked underneath. And it was just secured by the belt from Audrey's bathrobe.

I crossed my leg, got to keep my sprained ankle raised, and half turned away from his bedroom door so that the first thing that he saw when he came in was my bare legs and naked feet. I had just had a pedicure and my bright toenails shone in the firelight.

I knew that I looked sexy as hell.

I could hear the electric shower going. And I knew that Michael was in there naked as he took his shower.

My mouth is dry and my pulse fast, as I fantasize about what might happen. How he would burst into the room and profess his love for me. Before sweeping me up in his arms and kissing me long and deep.

I was feeling flushed. And not just from the roaring fire and the heavy fleece shirt.

Then the lights go out as the storm cuts the power.

Of course that meant the electric shower stopped as well.

There is still plenty of light from the roaring fire that Michael has lit, so I am not worried.

I hear Michael moving about inside his room.

Then some banging and a muffled curse.

But my jaw did hit the floor when Michael came charging into the room.

He is dripping wet, this time from the shower and not the storm. But still, his skin glistens in the firelight.

But he is also completely naked, with just a scrunched up towel hanging from his hand.

He has obviously jumped straight out of the shower and come running to rescue me again when the power went out.

He is once again hovering over me as I sit on the couch.

But this time he is naked.

Naked and aroused.

And I can not take my eyes off his hard cock.

I can not believe how big he is.

And thick.

So big and thick. And hard.

And throbbing lightly in the dancing firelight.

Fully exposed for me to see everything.

I lick my lips.

I know it sounds like a line from a dumb porno movie, but I genuinely lick my lips at the sight of his hard, throbbing cock.

I don't really hear what he says as he tries to wrap the towel around his waist. My head is buzzing and the towel does little to hide the straining cock that sticks out horizontally from his crotch.

I know that I have got to have it.

Got to have him.

I don't care anymore. I don't care if he thinks I'm too young. I don't care if he thinks I'm off limits because I'm his daughter's best friend. I don't care if he'll regret it afterward.

I just want him.

Even if it is just one night that he regrets forever, I want at least the memory of at least this one time.

I couldn't stop myself even if I wanted to.

And I don't want to stop.

I want him. Now.

Without any conscious thought or hesitation, my hand reaches out and grabs his hard shaft. I can feel its heat through the damp material of the towel that he is trying so badly in vain to cover himself with.

It feels hot, and hard, through the towel.

It feels alive in my hand. So full of life and vitality. Like it is its own living thing.

I pull the towel from his unresisting hands and let it drop onto the floor.

I never want anything to come between me and this magnificent cock ever again.

I want to gaze at it. And I want to touch it. And I want to taste it.

Taste the little drop of clear liquid slowly oozing from its tip.

Run my tongue and my lips up and down its length.

Feel its strength and power as I take it between my lips.

Feel its power as I take it deep.

Feel my power as I become everything for him.

The center of his world.

The only thing he wants to worship.

I can hear his ragged breathing. His whole body is rooted to the spot, unmoving, as I hold his cock in my hands. And yes, it takes two hands to hold it all.

My lips part for him as my tongue slips out and licks that little droplet.

It is sweet, and salty, and fresh.

"Oh, god," he moans, as his whole body starts to shake.

It is like an electric current is running through him. I can feel every fiber of his being ignite with desire.

His cock is literally pulsating in my hand as it slips into my mouth.

"No," he moans, a deep, deep moan.

I look up, making direct eye contact with him, and I feel him looking back into my very soul.

I am about to explode as I take him deeper into my mouth.

"No," he repeats, his hands finally moving to take hold of my head. "No," he breathes.

But I feel his hands hesitate between pulling me away and pulling my head right down to the base of his cock.

But then he is free and taking a step back from me.

I am filled with disappointment.

Filled with regret.

Filled with fear at what he might say.

But he doesn't say anything.

And he doesn't step away.

Instead with one swift movement he pushes me back onto the couch and is kneeling between my outstretched legs.

His head going straight to my pussy.

Automatically, and without hesitation, I grab his head with both my hands as a wave of pleasure erupts over me.

12 - Michael

I kneel between her legs.

Leaning forward.

The only thought in my mind is that I need to taste her.

Taste her essence.

Taste the source of the intoxicating aroma that has invaded my brain and made a zombie of me.

A zombie with just one thought.

A desire for just one thing

To consume her and make her mine.

Her touch on my cock had been thrilling.

The sensation of her lips and tongue as they grazed my sensitive flesh almost sent me over the edge.

And I so very much wanted to fall over that edge.

Wanted to ram my cock deep into her as my orgasm erupted.

But more than anything else I need to tase her.

To hold her essence on my tongue as her body erupts in orgasm around me.

Her soft flesh is compliant in my arms as I pull her thighs apart.

I lean forward and follow my nose to her center.

I lock my lips to her and start to feast.

Her legs lock around my head and her hands grab my skull and start to squeeze.

So tight

Ever so tight.

A ripple of convulsions race through her body.

And she moans.

A deep primeval moan. A moan that sends shivers through my own body.

I can feel every fiber of her flesh catch fire as my tongue finds her clit and I press into her throbbing nub.

She writhes on the couch. Her body twisting and turning, as her hands and legs squeeze around my head.

I am engulfed.

Engulfed in her flesh. Surrounded by her soft heat. Filled with the taste of her nectar. Reveling in the cascade of pleasure that I can feel running through her body.

It is all that I want. All that I have ever wanted. All that I want for the rest of my life.

But all good things must come to an end, eventually.

And eventually she is sated. Her body is limp. Her breathing ragged and horse. Her hands and thighs loose around my head.

But I am not finished yet.

I still have one more trick up my sleeve.

Something that I have been dreaming of for so many years.

And if my life is going to fall apart once this fantasy comes to a crashing halt against the reality of what we have done, then I want to have one memory. The cherry on top.

I slip my hands under her and bring her hips up, angling them slightly so I can have easy access as I slide my tongue down the length of her slit and find her entrance.

I lick around in small circles. Despite how wet she is, she is still ever so tight.

So tight she must be...

I moan, my cock pulsing untouched between my outspread thighs as the thought burns through my mind. The thought that I am her first.

She wiggles against me. A small giggle comes from her as I lick at her, still sensitive from her last orgasm.

I take a deep breath, steadying myself as I slowly press the tip of my tongue into her.

She is tight. Tight and hot. Squeezing around my tongue as I twist and lick, and slowly, but firmly, push deeper into her.

She opens around me. Allowing my tongue to penetrate her.

Her giggles turn to moans as her arousal starts to build once again.

I turn my tongue, twisting and probing as I start to search in earnest for my goal.

My tongue is long, and she is ever so tight around me as I lick upwards, lapping with my tongue.

"Ugh," she grunts, as I find the spot.

"Ugh. Ugh. Ugh." As I lap again and again. And again.

She moves around me, twisting her hips and grabbing my head once again. This time her thighs go wide as she pulls me hard against herself.

I pulse my tongue some more. Continuing to lap upwards at that special spot.

As she continues to grunt and grunt, and grunt some more.

Her grunts coming in time with my little tongue laps

Slowly, gradually, taking my time and not rushing things, I gently increase the pace of my lapping.

Her grunts merge into one long, continuous moan as her body goes rigid and all that exists for an eternity is the taste and feel of her innermost core on my tongue, and the long continuous moan that escapes her lips as an ocean of bliss carries her away.

And then the fucking landline rings.

13 - Emily

I don't know what is happening as reality comes crashing in all around me.

Suddenly I am empty and Michael is pulling away from me.

I try to hold on to him. But I have no strength in my hands. Or my legs. Or any part of my body, as I lie there on the couch like a discarded ragdoll.

For a moment I am confused, not realizing what has happened.

A strange ringing sound fills the air. A sound that I eventually recognise is a phone ringing.

An old fashioned landline phone.

The last few minutes had been bliss. I had finally gotten Michael just where I had always wanted him. But now this mundane, if antiquated, event has broken the spell.

I mean, who calls a landline in this day and age.

I open my eyes and moan in disappointment.

Michael is scrambling to his feet, muttering "Shit! Shit! Shit!" as he reaches out to the end table where the phone is.

And I am left abandoned and alone.

The dancing light from the fire still warms my body. But inside I am cold.

I want Michael back.

I want his touch.

I want his body.

I want him to claim me as his own, forever.

But instead the ringing stops and Michael breathes, "Hello?"

And I realize who must be on the other end of the line. Nobody except Audrey would be phoning this remote cabin.

"Oh, hi, Audrey," Michael says.

Then he listens. I can hear Audrey's faint voice on the other end, but I can't make out what she is saying.

"No, we are both ok," Michael replies.

Audrey says something.

Michael glances at me as he replies, "Emily hurt herself."

I can hear the concern in Audrey's voice.

"No, it is just a sprained ankle. She'll be right as rain in a few days."

Another concerned question.

"No, I'm sure," Michael replies. "It's not the first sprained ankle I've had to deal with."

I lie there on the couch, not even thinking of covering myself as I listen to his half of the conversation.

I am both stunned by the orgasms I have just had. And confused as to what might happen next.

I mean, I've had orgasms when I've masturbated before. But they were nothing compared to what I'd just experienced.

My body still felt like it was on fire.

But also reality was beginning to dawn.

I'd tasted forbidden fruit. I glanced at Michael, still naked and still hard.

I suppress a moan as my body tingles at the sight of his hefty cock.

He is rocking back and forth as he talks on the phone, and his cock is swinging gently from side to side.

It is almost hypnotic.

But I can not forget that on the other end of the telephone line is his daughter. My best friend. And now her father and I have crossed a line.

There can be no turning back.

I look up from his cock and catch his eye.

But he looks away before I can see how he feels.

I sit up on the couch and pull the shirt tight around myself.

His shirt.

The shirt I was wearing when he touched me for the first time.

The shirt I was wearing when anyone touched me for the first time.

I look back up at him. But he has turned his back to me as he continues to talk to his daughter on the phone.

But I cannot even register what he is saying.

All sorts of conflicting emotions and thoughts, feelings and desires, course through me. Yes, desire still runs through my veins.

I want to reach out and touch Michael.

I want to hold him again. To be held by him again. To feel him inside me. Not just his fingers touching me. Not just his tongue finding a spot I'd never found before.

I need to feel his thick, hard cock open me up as he pushes deep into me.

One part of me thinks that I am confused because I am a virgin. I have never done much with any boy. Because I have always wanted only one man. So maybe this is just some kind of normal reaction to my first time.

Michael was my first. That I could bring with me to my grave.

But I know from all the gossip and "girl talk" I've had over the years that it is not always like this for the first time.

I've heard lots of talk of first times. But I have never heard any girl talk of their heart splitting in two because the man they've desired for almost their entire lives was standing just a few feet away, but yet was somehow completely out of reach.

Then I realize that Michael has turned back to me.

I cannot help but look at his cock.

Perhaps for the very last time.

And I want nothing more than to feel it penetrate me.

But Michael is talking to me.

I look up, still not hearing what he is saying.

He is handling the telephone receiver to me.

"It's Audrey," he repeats.

"Um, yes." As I gather myself together. "Of course," I say, and I take the old fashioned phone from him.

He hands me the phone. I fumble for a moment with the unfamiliar handset. But I can not help but look at his hard cock still jutting out from his muscled body.

But suddenly reality is back as I put the handset to my ear.

"Oh, my god, Emily," Audrey says on the other end of the line.

My heart drops to my stomach. What does she know?

"You are going to be stuck all weekend in the cabin, alone with my father," Audrey continues.

"Em, yes," I try to keep my voice calm.

"You are going to be so bored," Audrey says.

"Um. It's not that bad," I reply, relief flooding through me.

She knows nothing of what has just happened.

I look up at Michael as Audrey continues to talk. But I cannot concentrate on her while her father is naked in front of me.

Not just her father, but the man I love.

He paces up and down a few times and I can't listen to Audrey. I try to keep my mind calm, what would Audrey think if she knew what her father and I had just been doing.

Could she accept it? Could she accept us?

I suddenly laugh as I realize I could be her stepmother.

"Are you even listening to me, Emily?" Audrey asks.

"Oh, sorry," I reply. "What was that?"

I listen as Audrey repeats some gossip about the boyfriend of a girl we both know being seen in a bar with another girl.

But while I make sympathetic noises, I can't really concentrate on the triviality of my former life.

Michael goes into his bedroom as Audrey continues with her story. Up to a few hours ago I would have been keenly interested in what she is saying.

But now it doesn't seem to matter at all.

I can hear Michael moving about in his room, draws and cupboards opening and closing.

I surmise he is getting dressed.

I hug myself as I listen to his daughter talk about my former life.

For that life is definitely over. No matter what happens I can't go back to being just his daughter's best friend.

Nothing can wipe away what has just happened between us.

I squeeze my thighs together as a shiver runs through my body. Even if what has happened is so incomplete.

I look at his bedroom door and I know that what has happened can't be the end of it.

His door opens.

I look up at him.

But he avoids my gaze.

Instead he heads straight for the door and leaves without saying a single word.

My heart feels as if it is going to burst through my chest.

I know that I need to hang up the phone and go after him.

But I can't let Audrey know anything is amiss

"Are you listening at all?" Audrey breaks in.

"Um, not really," I say.

"What?" Audrey asks.

"Your father gave me some painkillers for my ankle," I say. "And I think I'm pretty out of it."

"Ah, yes," Audrey replies. "My father has some pretty strong stuff in that emergency medical kit."

"I can barely keep my eyes open," I say. "I think I need to go to bed."

"Yes, you do that," Audrey says. "I'll call you first thing in the morning. Ok?"

"Ok, bye!" I say.

I hear her say, "goodbye." As I reach over and drop the receiver onto the base.

14 - Michael

I pace up and down a couple of times after I hand the phone to Emily.

I don't know what to do.

Should I stay?

Should I go?

I look at Emily.

She is sitting on the couch. Still wearing nothing except one of my shirts. Her face is flushed. Her hair bedraggled.

She is the most beautiful sight I have ever seen.

And yet she looks so shocked.

Traumatized even.

Staring off into space as she listens to my daughter talking on the phone.

Oh, my god! What have I done!

I turn and dash into my bedroom, shutting the door behind me.

I need to go.

I need to get out.

I can't face Emily.

Not after what I have done.

I freeze and stare at myself in the dresser mirror. Even in the dark I know how I must look.

How can I face my daughter Audrey?

I panic. I've got to go. I've got to get some space and clear my head.

I start to grab some clothes, quickly and randomly, and get dressed as fast as I can.

But as I am pulling up my jeans I am betrayed by my body yet again.

Why won't my dam cock go down?

I tuck it into my jeans and zip them up.

I can feel it squeezed against my thigh as I bend over to pull on my boots and tie my laces.

Then I face the bedroom door again. And I stop.

I can imagine Emily sitting on the couch, talking on the phone. Just outside my bedroom door.

I am going to have to face her.

I glance to my right, at the window.

No, I shake my head, and face the door again. I can't climb out the window.

Taking a deep breath I walk out, as quickly as I can without breaking into a run.

Outside Emily looks up at me. But I avoid what I know will be her accusing stare.

Trying my best to keep calm I walk out, softly closing the door behind me even as I want to run for the hills.

Outside I dash through the rain and sit into my truck, starting the engine and putting it into drive. And realize that I have nowhere to go.

With the bridge washed out, I am stuck on the mountain until the floodwaters subsided.

While there are several other cabins on the mountain I could go to, I don't know which would be worse. Finding cold, empty cabins or cabins full of life with their owners weathering the storm amongst friends and family.

I drop my head against the steering wheel and try to think.

I could drive down the mountain to the washed out bridge.

And what? Just sit there until they repair it. And do I just leave Emily here at the cabin?

I know the cabin is well stocked. But I can't just leave her here, alone.

But I can't go back inside to her.

Shame and doubt compete to be the dominant emotion in my heart.

But mostly I still feel desire. I still fucking want her. But there can be no way that she wants me.

I look up from the steering wheel and stare at the cabin.

The most beautiful, sweetest, most innocent girl is sitting in there talking with my daughter.

Oh, my god. Shame wins out. My daughter.

What on earth will she think of me?

Why could I not resist Emily for just one more night?

God knows I've had plenty of practice resisting my feelings for Emily for many, many years now.

Why did I have to slip up tonight?

Why did I have to destroy both my own and more importantly, Emily's life.

How can I ever face her again?

How can I face my daughter?

What is to become of me?

Of us?

No more just good friends.

This is not something that we can sweep under the rug and just never speak of again.

This is serious.

But then my feelings for Emily have always been serious.

How could they not be?

I know that she must surely hate me.

I look at the cabin once more and see the silhouette of Emily against the fire.

Is she moving about?

Surely she can't be walking. Not on her busted ankle.

But the door of the cabin opens. And the headlights of my truck clearly illuminate the scene as Emily stumbles through the door and starts to walk across the wet grass towards me.

But she doesn't get very far before her ankle gives way under her.

My blood runs cold at the thought of her being hurt once more and without thinking about it I am out of my truck and racing across the wet grass to pick her up.

15 - Emily

I have got to have him.

I don't know why he has left.

Why did he leave me?

But I know he hasn't gone very far

I can see the lights of Michael's truck outside

I can hear its engine running.

I can see the shadow of him in the cab.

But he is not moving.

The truck is still parked.

I half hop, half use the furniture for support as I make my way to the cabin door.

The only thing that slows me down is fumbling with the door handle.

I rush out after him, heedless of the rain that once again soaked me.

I know even my twisted ankle can't slow me down as I run towards his truck.

But my twisted ankle does slow me down.

Suddenly I am falling.

Falling through the rain and the dark night. The light from the truck's headlights blinding me.

And then I hit the ground with a soft squelch.

The grass under me is soaked, and the ground soft. So I am not hurt, apart from my already twisted ankle.

I start to push myself back up.

And suddenly I am lifted by a set of string arms.

"Michael?" I breathe.

"Emily," he replies.

"Where are you going?" I ask. "Why did you stop?"

"Stop?" He asks, holding me close.

His open coat is wrapped around me and my muddy skin sticks to his shirt. The heat from his body flowing into me.

"Why did you stop? Why did you leave?" My hands hold his head as I search for his face.

But he is silhouetted against the headlights and I can not read his expression.

"I had to," he says. "The phone."

"Yes, Audrey," I reply. But I don't want to think about Audrey right now.

"But Michael," I say. Didn't he love me?

"I had to leave," he says. "I wouldn't have been able to stop myself."

"Stop yourself?" I ask.

"You're so beautiful. So kind and loving," he replies. "And now I've gone and ruined everything."

"Ruined everything?" I start to laugh as relief floods through me. "You haven't ruined anything." I kiss him. A quick peck. But right in his lips. "You've made everything perfect," I say.

"Perfect?" He looks at me. "But I... we... What I did?"

"What we did," I say. I kiss him again. "I have wanted this for years," I say.

"Wanted this?"

"Wanted this and more," I say. "I have always loved you. Even before I knew what love was."

"You love me?" He replies.

And I swear that there are tears mixed with the rain running down his face.

"You love me?" He repeats.

"Of course I love you," I say.

"You love me."

"Yes," I reply. "I fucking love you."

I bring my hands down and unbuckle his belt. I can feel his hard cock straining against the material as I pull his jeans open and reach inside.

Once again I am holding his hard cock.

I can feel him almost throbbing in my hand.

"I love you," he says.

And I squeeze the shaft of his cock as hard as I can as a shiver of excitement runs through me.

I lift my head and our lips meet, open. And our tongues intertwine.

I try to pull his jeans down with my left hand, because I am never letting go of his cock now that I've got a grip on it again.

But I can't get his jeans to move down.

He wraps his arms around my body, one big hand cupping my bottom, the other between my shoulders, as he lifts me up a little and gently lays me down in the wet grass.

The shirt that I am wearing is completely soaked through and the ground is wet and cold under me.

But he is on top of me and the heat from his body is like a furnace.

He reaches down and pulls his jeans off his hips.

I gasp into his mouth as his cock is finally free.

I try to guide it down between my legs, but there isn't enough room.

I can feel him laugh as we continue to kiss and he lifts his hips up.

His cock leaves a hot trail across my skin as I try to get it positioned where I want it.

But my aim is bad and I hit my clitoris.

I shudder and shake as an orgasm rips through my body.

He presses hard against me as two, three, and then four waves of pleasure wash over me.

It is good. But it is not enough.

And more importantly I have lost my grip on his cock.

I feel him growl as he reaches down and puts his cock where I want it, sliding its head between my lips as he presses against my entrance.

I feel my breath leave me as he starts to push in.

I can not form words.

I can not form thoughts.

I can't even feel the wet grass anymore as he starts to fill me.

Opening me and pushing into me.

I can feel my legs quiver as he pushes in deep.

Deep, where no man has ever gone before.

My arms cling to his shoulders.

His body presses me into the soft earth.

It feels so right.

It feels perfect.

Everything is still for a moment.

Then he starts to move and my understanding of perfection undergoes a complete transformation as my breath, no, my very soul, is sucked from my body.

He moves so perfectly.

Filling my need. Making me complete as my heart and body overflow with fulfillment.

Epilogue- Emily

Waking up this morning next to Michael feels just as special as waking up next to him that first morning in the cabin.

Not that we did much sleeping that first night. But we've spent every night together since.

The bulk of him lying next to me makes me sleep like a baby.

And speaking of babies. I run my hand over my swelling belly, and laugh as I feel our son kick.

"How do you feel?" Michael asks.

I smile at him and lean in for a kiss. "Like the luckiest girl in the world," I say.

My husband smiles as his child kicks again.

I grab Michael's hand and press it to my belly.

"Oh, he's wide awake this morning," Michael says in wonder.

I love Michael's smile. I love making him smile.

And he loves making me happy.

I look across the room at the bassinet, with the animal mobile hanging over it, ready for our first child.

Michael has spent the past six months since our wedding making both the house and the cabin childproof in every way.

I keep telling him that Michael jr. won't be crawling for months.

But Michael wants everything ready.

He's like a first time expectant dad.

And by the way Michael jr. is kicking up a fuss this morning. I don't think he's going to wait the six weeks until his due date to come into this world.

A world made perfect by the presence of his father.

At first, Aubrey had been very upset. Having her father hook up with her best friend was quite a shock to her.

But once I convinced her that her father did nothing wrong and that we were both serious, she gave us her blessing. As long as she could be maid of honor at our wedding.

Which she was.

Which was not long in coming.

Not just because I got pregnant that first night in the cabin. But because neither Michael nor myself saw any reason to wait a minute longer than we had to.

We had both waited long enough.

My father had "come back from the brink" finding a new lease of life as I had planned my wedding with Michael. He is now six months sober, and looking forward to becoming a grandfather. He's even started seeing the widow who lives next door to him. So who knows what might happen there.

All in all, I am the luckiest girl in the world.

I push Michael onto his back and start kissing my way down his perfect body.

"Oh, no, I have to..." but his voice cuts off with a deep sigh as my mouth finds its goal.

He is my first, and my last. And I am his everything.

Visit www.AbiLeix.com for eMail signup.

Did you love *Together at the Cabin - With My Best Friend's Father*? Then you should read *Together at the Coffee Shop - With my Best Friend's Father*[1] by Alara Knight!

Nothing will ever be the same again.

EmmaHe keeps coming into the Coffee Shop where I work. The man of my dreams. The man I have always wanted.But I know my love is forlorn. He is the father of my best friend.But why does he tease me so?

JoshuaShe is much too young for me. And totally out of my league.So why do I keep coming back to her?I've managed to control myself all this time.But tonight when we are alone together for the first time...

---

1. https://books2read.com/u/4j7a0l

2. https://books2read.com/u/4j7a0l

This book is a standalone romance novella featuring an Older Man and a Younger Woman(OMYW). It is a sweet and "safe" (no cheating) short story that builds to a very steamy climax and a guaranteed HEA.

Read more at https://reamstories.com/alaraknight.

Also by Alara Knight

Halloween Heat
Caught on Halloween Night

Punished: Volume 1
Punished by Her Cowboy
Punished by Her Professor
Punished by Her Sheriff
Punished by Mr. Ward
Punished: Volume 1

Together Forever
Together at the Cabin - With My Best Friend's Father
Together In The Caribbean - With My Best Friend's Father
Together After the Party - With my Best Friends Father
Together at the Coffee Shop - With my Best Friend's Father
Together at the Beach House - With My Best Friend's Father

Standalone

Kissing the Bride-To-Be's Daddy

Watch for more at https://reamstories.com/alaraknight.

About the Author

Alara Knight is a writer of erotica, and erotic romance, who focuses on older men and younger women. She is passionate about storytelling and enjoys creating worlds for her readers to escape into. Her stories are full of twists and turns, and you never know what might happen next. She is always open to feedback and suggestions, so please don't hesitate to get in touch.

Alara writes steamy, sexy stories, which include age gap, virgin, best friend's father, and so much more!

Check out her Ream author page for free stories.

Follow her there for more free stories, and news of new books and promotions.

Read more at https://reamstories.com/alaraknight.